Charlie and Grandma

Charlie and Grandma

by Sally G. Ward

SCHOLASTIC INC.

New York Toronto London Auckland Sydney

ISBN 0-590-33954-0

Copyright © 1986 by Sarah G. Ward.
All rights reserved. Published by Scholastic Inc.
Art direction by Diana Hrisinko
Book design by Theresa Fitzgerald

12 11 10 9 8 7 6 5 4 3 2 1   9   6 7 8 9/8 0 1/9

Printed in the U.S.A.   10

For Ken, with love

Grandma, I'm hungry.
I'm going to get myself an apple.

Charles, you wait up. I'll be there in a minute.

Charles, I hope you are being
a good boy in there....

I'm almost done.

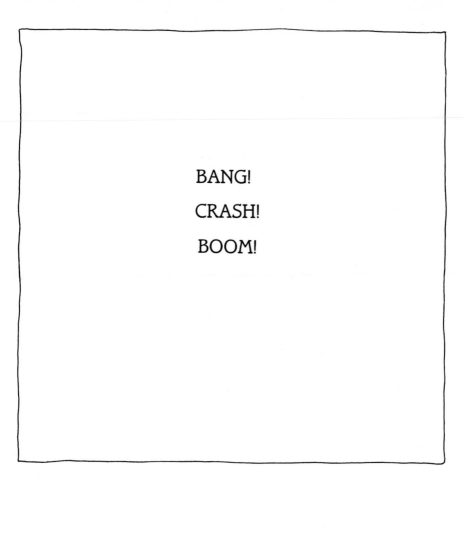

Look, Grandma! I got an apple all by myself!

The end.